For Lindsey, the first one to love this book.

Text and Illustrations copyright ©2018 by Christopher Tully Bloodworth.
You can see more of his work on his website at christophertullybloodworth.com.
All rights reserved.

This book was typeset in Marion, with text layout by Sarah Elmore. You can see more of her work on her website
at sarahelmore.com.
Illustrations were drawn with ink and brushpen, and colored digitally using Procreate® and Waterlogue® on iPad.

Published by Sliding Shelf Press
Birmingham, AL
slidingshelfpress.com

ISNB 978-1-7323515-1-6

First edition, 2018

A Girl and her Bear

Written and Illustrated by
Christopher Tully Bloodworth

Sliding Shelf Press
BIRMINGHAM, ALABAMA

Not too far

from where they lived in the wood,
A girl and her bear walked along as one should:

Taking in sights
      of the blossoms of spring,
And all of the creatures such good weather brings.

So though they ought to've had fun on that day,
The girl couldn't think of **one game** they could play.

"I'm bored," she told Bear.
"There's nothing to do.
I'm so bored, I can't think of anything new."

"There're only two options as I can see:
Play inside or out, and **neither suits me.**"

Now Bear loved the girl with all of his heart,
So he pondered how he might change her mind
—just in part.

"Hold on," he said, "I think you've missed something. Play 'Inside or out'? But that's **everything!**

"In just those two places, we can create
Whole worlds worth exploring
and thrills that await.

"We could sail far across the ocean wide,
Discovering **new islands** to explore.

"But if we get sick from the sea's wavy tide,
We could be safely back home before four.

"We could think up something
simple and fun
Like getting some ice cream for us to share.

"But then,
    as you know, I'd need to wash up
Because bears must be **handled with care.**

"So you see, we could do most **anything**,
And I would not care a bit what it was.

As long as I'm with you
and you're with me,

Together, we'll be happy
just because."

"You're right!" said the girl,
and she took his paw in hand.

So then the two ran off to see
all far and distant lands.

They first climbed high Mount Everest's peak,

Before tumbling down its snowy sides.

sniff
sniff

And then they played some
hide-and-seek,

But Bear could really hide!

Next they went to the vast Grand Canyon
And, **scared**, peered carefully
over the edge.

"Oh no!" said the girl. "There's **no way** to cross!"
"Hmmm," thought Bear,
　　　"could we just **build a bridge?**"

So using just sticks from the woods
    by their home,

They built a **great bridge**
and continued to roam.

All over the world,
they **walked**...

... and they **trekked**

'Till the girl and her bear were so tired they slept.

As they slept, they **dreamed** of all of the things that they'd done and had yet to do

Until it was late and their mother went out to find them in a place that she knew.

Because, of course,
they hadn't really left their wood.
For adventures like that,
you'd need a guide!

Still, your imagination is just as good...

When you have **a good friend** by your side.